Let's Explore Australia

by Elle Parkes

I0878473

BUMBA BOOKS™

LERNER PUBLICATIONS ◆ MINNEAPOLIS

Note to Educators:

Throughout this book, you'll find critical thinking questions. These can be used to engage young readers in thinking critically about the topic and in using the text and photos to do so.

Copyright © 2018 by Lerner Publishing Group, Inc.

All rights reserved. International copyright secured. No part of this book may be reproduced, stored in a retrieval system, or transmitted in any form or by any means—electronic, mechanical, photocopying, recording, or otherwise—without the prior written permission of Lerner Publishing Group, Inc., except for the inclusion of brief quotations in an acknowledged review.

Lerner Publications Company
A division of Lerner Publishing Group, Inc.
241 First Avenue North
Minneapolis, MN 55401 USA

For reading levels and more information, look up this title at www.lernerbooks.com.

Library of Congress Cataloging-in-Publication Data

Names: Parkes, Elle, author.
Title: Let's explore Australia / by Elle Parkes.
Description: Minneapolis : Lerner Publications, [2018] | Series: Bumba books—Let's explore countries | Includes bibliographical references and index.
Identifiers: LCCN 2016041007 (print) | LCCN 2016041153 (ebook) | ISBN 9781512433623 (library bound : alkaline paper) | ISBN 9781512455557 (paperback : alkaline paper) | ISBN 9781512450385 (eb pdf)
Subjects: LCSH: Australia—Juvenile literature.
Classification: LCC DU96 .P374 2018 (print) | LCC DU96 (ebook) | DDC 994—dc23

LC record available at https://lccn.loc.gov/2016041007

Manufactured in the United States of America
2-46331-23868-7/16/2018

LERNER SOURCE™

Expand learning beyond the printed book. Download free, complementary educational resources for this book from our website, www.lerneresource.com.

Table of Contents

A Visit to Australia 4

Map of Australia 22

Picture Glossary 23

Read More 24

Index 24

A Visit to Australia

Australia lies between two oceans.

It is a big island.

It is below Asia.

Australia has dry deserts.

It has many hills.

Rain forests cover

other areas.

Koalas live in forests.

They sleep in trees.

They eat leaves.

Why do you think koalas eat leaves?

Kangaroos also live in Australia.

Mother kangaroos have pouches.

They carry their babies in them.

Australia has small towns

and big cities.

Many people live in cities.

Sydney is one of the

biggest cities.

Many people visit Australia.

They dive at the Great Barrier Reef.

They see fish and coral.

What other sea creatures might you see at the Great Barrier Reef?

Many Australian foods

use meat.

A popular dish is meat pie.

It is meat and gravy

in a crust.

Cricket is a top sport.

It is a bit like baseball.

Many people play or watch cricket.

How is cricket similar to baseball?

Australia is a beautiful place.

There are many things to see.

Would you like to go to Australia?

Map of Australia

Picture Glossary

coral

underwater structures made of sea creatures

cricket

a sport played with a bat and a ball

deserts

dry places that get little rain

rain forests

thick, tropical forests where lots of rain falls

Read More

Oachs, Emily Rose. *Australia*. Minneapolis: Bellwether, 2016.

Parkes, Elle. *Let's Explore Kenya*. Minneapolis: Lerner Publications, 2018.

Perkins, Chloe. *Australia*. New York: Simon Spotlight, 2017.

Index

cricket, 18

deserts, 7

Great Barrier Reef, 14

kangaroos, 11

koalas, 8

meat pie, 17

rain forests, 7

Sydney, 12

Photo Credits

The images in this book are used with the permission of: © narvikk/iStock.com, p. 5; © Stanislav Fosenbauer/Shutterstock.com, pp. 6–7, 23 (bottom left); © Signature Message/Shutterstock.com, p. 9; © idiz/Shutterstock.com, p. 10; © Jason Ho/Shutterstock.com, pp. 12–13; © JonMilnes/Shutterstock.com, pp. 15, 23 (top left); © Joe Gough/Shutterstock.com, pp. 16–17; © PeopleImages/iStock.com, pp. 19, 23 (top right); © razihusin/iStock.com, pp. 20–21; © AustralianCamera/Shutterstock.com, p. 23 (bottom right).

Front Cover: © Alan L Meakin/Shutterstock.com.